Contents

The Acts of Union
1

A Nation
Again
5

Life in Eighteenth-century Scotland
72

The Acts of
Union

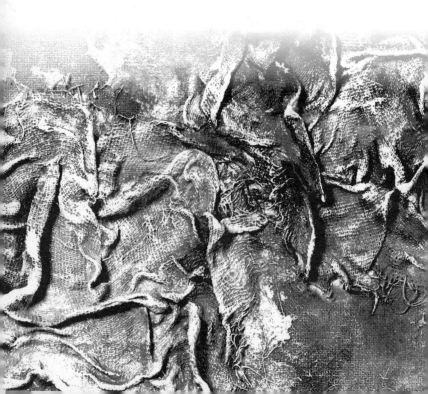

This story is about Annie, who might have been born in 1690 or thereabouts. There is no record of her existence, because ordinary people who are not rich or famous don't get written about in their own time. She's a might-have-been.

The things that happen to Annie in the story happened to many people at that time, and the men she meets in Edinburgh were real and true. The letters they wrote still exist, and their faces look at us from portraits and engravings.

The arguments that raged in Scotland three hundred years ago are still hotly debated today, and it is as though Fletcher and Lockhart, Queensberry, Hamilton and Mar still walk among us. People with great ideas never completely die – their opinions live on.

Annie and her father live, as well, in the Scots of today whose everyday lives, whether they know it or not, form a small part of history.

A Nation Again

1

On a sunless June morning in 1699, Annie Weir climbed
the hill behind the little houses of Maxwellheugh. Her
bare feet were as tough as a dog's paws, used to the
roughness of heather and stone, but her legs were trem-
bling a little, and her head felt dizzy. She was very
hungry – so hungry that a constant pain cramped her
stomach and made her limbs ache.

At the top of the slope, she stopped beside the black-
thorn bush to look down at the huddle of small roofs below
her. The ridges of earth that should have been green with
barley and oats were nothing but brown mud. This was
the third year running when terrible weather had ruined

the crops, and in this past winter the choice had been stark – eat the precious seed-corn saved for the spring sowing, or starve.

For some, there had been no choice at all. Annie thought of her sister, Sarah, whose curly dark hair and bright smile she would never see again, and of the baby born last October, a little boy they called Ian, whose life had lasted only three days. Why did I live, and not them? she wondered now. Annie herself was a skinny thing for a girl of nearly nine, but somehow she stayed alive. 'My wee sparrow' her mother called her. But a strong sparrow, perhaps.

Annie's mother was ill. Yesterday, she had babbled about milking the cow and feeding the whey to the pig when the cheese had been made, forgetting that the animals had been killed and eaten long ago. However, when Annie came out this morning in search of food, her mother had been more peaceful, making no sound except for the hesitant gasp of her breath.

'See what you can find, lassie,' Annie's father had said

as he set off for the town of Kelso that lay across the river. He'd heard that there was Poor Relief to be had there – a little money and a bag of oatmeal.

Oatmeal. Annie's mouth watered at the thought of a bowl of warm porridge, and her empty stomach cramped painfully. Every day for weeks now, she had searched the hill for anything edible, peeling the bark from silver birch trees and gathering any green leaves that smelled as if they could be eaten. There were no berries yet on the brambles or rowan or wild rose, but she picked their blossoms sometimes for their faint, honeyed taste.

Today, she could easily have lain down in the heather and gone to sleep, not caring much if she never woke. But what if her father came back empty-handed? Annie knew she must not sleep. She moved carefully across the hill, scanning each leaf and twig and tree root as intently as a bird.

Late the same afternoon, Annie made her way triumphantly back to the farmtoun, clutching an armful of wild parsnip root and dragging a stag's fallen antler which had laid half-hidden in the bracken. Chopped up and boiled, it would give a hint of flavour to a broth.

She saw that her father was back from Kelso – but he stood outside their one-roomed house among a group of people, and as Annie approached, she heard one of them say, 'Ye cannae blame yourself, Tam. She'd have died whether you were here or no'.'

Tam nodded dumbly. Then he saw Annie, and made his way towards her. He put both hands on her shoulders, gripped gently as if to hold her together. Then he said in a voice rough with unshed tears, 'Well, my lassie. My wee sparrow. We're on our own.' Then he held her close as tears began to pour down Annie's face, and the branching antler lay on the ground unnoticed.

In the days that followed, Annie did her best to fill the huge gap left by her lost mother. She kept the little one-roomed dwelling clean as best she could, and cooked the oatmeal her father had been given in Kelso. The food made her feel stronger in spite of her grief, but Tam was silent and unhappy. Every day he went to the town in search of work, for he was a skilled carpenter as well as being capable of all farm work – but the landowners had made no profit in the three hard years when there had been no crops or stock to sell. Nobody was taking on workers, not even to replace the many who had died of starvation and sickness. But one day, Tam came back fired with excitement.

'There's another fleet of ships going out to South America,' he said. 'To Darien, the new Scottish trading-post. The first went three years ago. That would have been 1696. They're needing able-bodied men.'

Annie stared at him. Where was South America? It sounded even further than Glasgow. 'Will I go, too?' she asked.

Tam shook his head. 'Best not, Annie. There's some wives and children out there, right enough, but it's a long way, across a great ocean, and I don't know what we'll find. We've heard no news yet from the first settlers.'

We, thought Annie. Her father was already a member of these adventurers, at least in his mind.

'It's a great chance, Annie,' Tam went on, his face lit up with enthusiasm. 'The nobles and big land-owners have set up the Company of Scotland, to get our share of the overseas trade. And about time – the English have hogged it for too long.'

Annie nodded, although she didn't understand. She hardly liked to put the question that troubled her. 'Will I stay here on my own?'

Tam laughed, ruffling her curly dark hair. 'No, lassie – you'll go to your Auntie Margaret in Kelso. Her man's a blacksmith. He still has a good trade, shoeing the horses of the gentry.'

But Auntie Margaret and Uncle Robert had five children, Annie thought, all of them younger than her. Surely they would not want another mouth to feed? 'When are you going?' she asked.

'Soon. The ship sails from Leith docks in ten days' time.

That's by Edinburgh. It's a long walk to get there.' His eyes were restless, and Annie could see he was impatient to get started. 'We'll be a power in the world at last,' he said. Then he looked at Annie and his face fell a little. 'I know it's hard, wee sparrow, but what am I to do? There's nothing here but begging and hardship, and at least this way we've a good chance. The noblemen who put their money into Darien know what they're doing. They built the ships, hired the men, drew the maps – there's half of all the money in Scotland in this scheme. Four hundred thousand pounds, Annie. Just imagine that! We're all going to make our fortunes.'

Annie nodded, unable to speak.

Her father put a finger under her chin and made her look at him. 'Listen,' he said. 'Always remember, you are as good as anyone else. The rich and powerful are not better than us, just luckier. It's a matter of chance, that's all. But I have a chance now, and I'm going to take it.'

Annie nodded again, and swallowed hard, suppressing her threatened tears. If he could be brave, then so could she.

2

Living with Margaret and Robert was not as bad as Annie had feared. Her aunt was a kindly, happy woman, and Annie enjoyed helping to look after the younger children. The biggest ones, Kate and Jenny, willingly made room for Annie to share their bed, and George, the baby, reminded her of the wee brother she so nearly had.

For the first time, Annie went to school, together with Kate and Jenny, each of them carrying a slab of peat, as all the children did, for the schoolroom fire. The school was no more than a single-roomed building tucked beside the wall of the old Abbey, but it was the biggest place Annie had ever been in. Her parents' home had been barely six paces from wall to wall, and Margaret's was not much bigger, although they did have an extra room as well as the smithy itself.

At school, the children sat side by side on long benches, youngest at one end and the older ones at the other, and Mr Lockhart, the dominie, was patient unless anyone was inattentive or made a noise. Annie never made a noise. She was fascinated by the letters she copied on to her slate, murmuring their sounds in the silence of her mind, and after a few weeks, they were suddenly joining themselves into words that spoke to her like a real, invisible person. Soon she caught up with the older ones who were learning Latin.

'This is the father of the English language, Annie,' Mr Lockhart explained, 'and Greek is its mother, with uncles and aunts from the lands of the Celts and the Vikings. Once you know this family, our language will make beautiful sense to you – but first you must work hard, and put up with some boredom.'

Sometimes when heads drooped and eyes closed over

the hard work, Mr Lockhart would say it was time for a song and a story. Annie loved this. She knew dozens of tunes and countless verses. 'Ca' The Yowes', 'Queen Mary's Lament', 'Galla Water', 'My Nanie O' – their melodies ran in her mind like secret happiness. She found herself enjoying her life in Kelso, although she prayed every night for her father, away in the place called Darien.

A year or more passed, and then at Easter Mr Lockhart went on a visit to Edinburgh. One night shortly afterwards, he came to Robert and Margaret's house.

'Please come in,' said Margaret, curtseying and flustered at having the dominie at her door.

Robert got up from the fire and said, 'I hope my children have not been misbehaving.'

'Not at all,' said Mr Lockhart. 'They're good children. No, I came to tell you that three ships have come back from Darien. All Edinburgh is talking about it. And I believe your brother, Tam –'

'Is he home?' Annie asked excitedly, and was frowned at by Robert and Margaret for interrupting.

Mr Lockhart didn't frown. 'I don't know, Annie,' he said. 'Let us hope so. But the news is not good.' His face was grave. 'These three ships are all that have returned from the twenty or more that went out. It seems that Darien is a place of fever-ridden swamps, impossible for northern people like ourselves to live in. Our settlers were plagued with sickness – and the ships did not carry the supplies they needed.'

Margaret slipped an arm round Annie's shoulders as they listened.

'The native people there were friendly,' the dominie went on, 'but the Spanish were a different matter. They claimed that Darien was theirs – though Heaven knows, they did little enough with it in all the years they called it their own. They attacked our people and were bravely driven off, then attacked again. And our King William,' his face darkened further, 'showed his true English colours,

Dutchman though he is. The English colonies in America and the Caribbean would have sent troops to help defend Darien, but His Majesty forbade it.'

'Why?' Annie gasped. 'Isn't he the king of Scotland as well as England?'

Nobody reproved her this time. 'He is indeed,' agreed Mr Lockhart. 'But the English will not let Scotland have any power. Even though we are so few and so poor, they fear us. They fancy that we are all wild Highlanders, feuding and cattle-raiding and speaking a language the English cannot understand.' He gave a small shrug. 'It's true, of course, that the king is not much loved here. Why should he be, when the MacDonalds of Glencoe were cut to pieces simply for being late in swearing loyalty to him? I for one would like to see the rightful descendent of our Scottish King James on the throne, James Edward Stuart. The Latin for James is Jacobus, Annie, hence we supporters of James Edward are called Jacobites.'

'Yes,' said Annie. The Jacobite songs she had heard in

the streets of Kelso were part of her store of music – but there was more to worry about than Latin words. Her father might be dead.

As if thinking the same thing, Margaret asked, 'Do you know, sir, how many people have returned? And how many – have not?'

'About three hundred have come back,' said the dominie. 'Most of them from the second expedition, so there is every hope for Tam. When they saw the scale of the disaster, they came straight home with those who were still alive. But over two thousand are lost.'

'Two thousand people,' said Robert, stunned. 'And all those fine ships. Whatever happened? They were sunk by Spanish guns, I suppose.'

'And by storm, and by the weakness of sick, exhausted crewmen.' Mr Lockhart shook his head. 'This will ruin Scotland. Half of our total wealth is lost for ever. We are bankrupt.'

'God help us all,' said Robert.

When Annie was coming home from school a few days later, a woman stopped her. 'There was somebody asking for you, lassie.'

Annie gasped. 'My father?'

'He didnae say. He's one of the drovers, going down to England with a herd of cattle. But he asked for you by name. You'll find him down by the river. They rest the beasts there overnight, on the meadows.'

Annie rushed home and poured out her news.

'I'll come with you,' said Robert.

What seemed an ocean of black cattle was settling itself on the grass in the fading light of evening. A dog barked as Robert and Annie approached, and a man looked up from the group round the fire. Like the others, he was wrapped in the dirty tartan plaid of the Highlander, and his bare legs and unkempt hair gave Annie a twinge of fear. These were the wild men from the north, fighters and – so people said – marauders.

'One of you was asking for Annie Weir of

Maxwellheugh,' said Robert.

There was a mutter of Gaelic among the drovers, most of whom had not understood Robert's words, then the man who had looked up got to his feet.

'Tam of Maxwellheugh says he is home now.' The English words came to him uncertainly, but he had memorised the message well. 'He is to Midlothian, to find work as a miner. When he has money, he will send for you.'

Annie nodded eagerly, her eyes fixed on the man's weather-beaten face.

'Did he say anything else?' Robert asked.

The drover shook his head. 'That is what he told me.' Then he added, 'You are a farrier, they say. Some of the beasts are lame – will you look at them?'

One favour deserved another. 'It may be they need shoes on the outer half of the foot,' Robert said. 'The road is rough for them, and it's a long way.'

Annie followed her uncle as he moved with the drover among the cattle, her fear of the unkempt men forgotten in the joy of the message they had brought her. Tam had never learned to read and write, but he seemed close now. And this year, the spring had been warm and kind. Maybe the worst was over.

3

Summer came, and Annie heard nothing more from Tam. The days shortened into autumn and a harvest of sorts was gathered, though there had been little seed-corn to sow. The winter would be another hungry one. Everybody knew now about Darien, and the shame of it added a new and terrible weight to what people called 'King William's ill years'.

In October, Robert was kicked on the knee by a bad-tempered horse. Margaret bathed the swollen wound and wrapped it in clean rags, but Robert said after feeling it with skilled fingers, 'There's a bone broken.' He was right. Despite Margaret's poultices, the knee became infected, and within three days Robert was in a high fever. A weight of dread hung over the house. Annie thought of the way Robert stood while shoeing a horse, his legs flexed as he bent over the hoof held between his knees, and knew that even if he survived the fever, there was little chance that he would work as a farrier again.

At school, Annie worried and could not pay attention. She was ten years old now, going on eleven, and although she wasn't tall – she would never be that – she was wiry and strong after Margaret's food and care, well able to work. She ought not to be sitting here learning Latin, she thought. She should be earning money. But there was no work to be had in Kelso, where even grown men long skilled in a trade were begging in the streets. That's why her father had gone to work in the mines instead of coming back here.

When the other children went out, Annie paused at the dominie's desk.

'Mr Lockhart, do children work in coal mines?'

'Indeed they do, Annie. Quite young children.' He shook his head with disapproval. 'They start at only six years old, I've heard. It makes a mockery of our fine education laws. No child should be slaving in the dust and the dark – they should be in school.'

'Yes,' said Annie vaguely. Her thoughts were spinning.

Mr Lockhart looked at her in concern. 'Is anything the matter, my dear?'

'No sir.' *They start at only six years old*. 'Thank you, sir.'

On her way home, Annie saw that the drovers were in the town again, but thought nothing of it. Many droves of cattle had been through in the six months since the message from her father, but there had been no further word. She went into the house – and Margaret turned from Robert's bedside to smile at her. 'There's something for you,' she said. 'Look on the table.'

A small leather purse lay there, and when Annie picked it up, she could feel coins slip and clink inside it.

'From your father,' said Margaret. 'The drover brought it.'

'What did he say?' Annie asked eagerly. 'Is my father well? When will I see him?'

Margaret's smile faded. 'The drover said he looked poorly,' she admitted. 'He has a bad cough – maybe it's some foreign sickness from that God-forsaken place. But he'll be all right, don't you worry.'

Annie turned away, fingering the purse that Tam's hands had held. She knew now why her thoughts of working had been so insistent. Her father needed her.

'No, Annie, no!' Margaret was horrified. 'A young lassie like you, journeying all that way? You may not even find Tam, and as to working with him – you're not to think of it.'

Robert looked across from his bed. The fever had broken a few nights ago and he was no longer in the grip of wild dreams, but he was weak and exhausted, and still in great pain.

'We'll manage, lassie,' he said, his voice hardly more than a whisper. 'You're no' a burden to us, dinnae think that.'

'There's no need for you to go,' Margaret agreed. 'You're part of our family, my dear, you belong here.'

Annie felt her eyes prick with tears as she smiled at these people who had been so kind to her. But if she herself was to be kind in return, she must take no more from them. In bed that night, snug beside Kate and Jenny for the last time, she prayed for them – and for herself, in the frightening days that lay ahead.

She got up before dawn and dressed quietly, bundling her few clothes in an old shawl. Working by touch in the darkness, she tipped the coins into her hand and put them silently one by one on the table, returning a single one to the purse to take with her. The rest would help with the hard times that were coming to Robert and Margaret. Then she let herself out into the starlit morning.

On the grass by the river, the black cattle were still lying down, and the drovers slept beside them for the warmth of their sheltering bodies. One man was up, crouching by the newly rekindled fire as he fed it with small sticks, his plaid swathed round him in the chill of the morning. He looked up at Annie and smiled. 'You are early about,' he said.

Annie came a little closer. 'I'm going to Midlothian,' she told him. 'To be with my father.'

'The miner.'

'Yes! Do you know him?'

The drover shook his head. 'Only that we brought a message from him once before.'

'Oh. I thought you might know where I could find him.' But even as she spoke, Annie knew it was a silly idea. These men had no knowledge of the Lowlands. They followed the rough roads worn by the feet of their cattle, pausing at night to rest their beasts, but for them, it was as though they travelled through a foreign country.

'The mining places are by Penicuik,' the man said, trying to help her. 'Rosewell, they say. Bonnyrigg, Loanhead. We do not come through them.'

'Which way should I go?' Annie asked. *Rosewell*, *Bonnyrigg*, *Loanhead*. She must remember these names. *Penicuik*.

The drover waved an arm. 'North, towards Falkirk. But turn off at West Linton.'

It sounded simple. Above the dark shape of the hills, grey daylight was starting to appear. Margaret and the children would be getting up. 'I'd best be going,' Annie said.

The man laid some more twigs on the fire, then glanced up. 'God guard you, lassie,' he said. And, in the Catholic faith of most Highlanders, he made the sign of the cross.

7

The days that followed merged into an endless dream of treading in the broad pattern of hoof-prints that led across the moor. Sometimes the going was rough and stony, but often Annie's bare feet sank deep in a soft morass of dung and mud. There were few people on the road now that the big drove had gone through, but the travellers Annie met would always stop to exchange news. Often they would share a bit of bannock, and the solid goodness of oatmeal dough baked on a girdle filled her stomach with a warmth that lasted a comfortably long time. She spent the nights curled up wherever she could find shelter – in the lee of a big rock for preference, with an armful of dry bracken for bedding.

Late on the afternoon of the third day, Annie came to West Linton. Ahead of her, the band of trodden ground went on up the hill to a pass between two peaks. Cauld Stane Slap, the travellers had told her. And to her right, a track snaked down across the moor to a distant river.

'Aye, Penicuik's down there,' a tinker woman said in answer to Annie's question. 'And Edinburgh, if that's where you're wanting.' Then she was off up the hill with her husband and children, their tied bundles of tin pans and kettles clinking like goatbells.

Darkness came early because of the grey, heavy sky, and rain began to fall. As she came down the hill, Annie could no longer see the roofs of Penicuik, and there was no cottage or byre where she could find shelter. She came past a group of trees that grew by the river – then stopped and stared. A light was shining ahead of her, quite high up. She climbed a low stone wall and made her way up sloping grass, sheep-nibbled, and saw that the light came from tall windows in a great house. As she gazed, music began to sound in the lit room, and it had a tinkling delicacy she had never heard before. Like someone hypnotised, she went on towards it, and stared through the rain-streaked glass.

A young man was sitting at an instrument, his fingers moving quickly over its ivory keys. He began to sing, and Annie gave a quick breath of laughter as she recognised the tune of 'Bide Ye Yet'. The verse ended, and he looked up and saw her.

Annie dared not move. The young man's eyes met her gaze and held it as he got up. He opened the long window and stared at her.

'What do you want?' he asked.

'Nothing.' Annie looked past him at the silver candlesticks and glossy furniture, and felt ashamed to be so wet and dirty.

'I'm sorry – I'll go now.' She turned away, but he took a step forward and touched her arm.

'No, wait,' he said. 'Where do you come from?'

'Maxwellheugh, sir, near Kelso. But –'

'*Kelso?* And you've walked from there?'

'Yes, sir. Then I heard the music.'

'Do you like music?'

'Oh, yes, sir.' Annie forgot her embarrassment. 'I know the tune you were playing, sir, it's 'Bide Ye Yet'.'

'So it is,' he agreed, then added impetuously, 'Come in and sing it for me. It needs a girl's voice.'

'But –'

'Never mind.' Despite her wet clothes and dirty bare feet, he led her across the soft carpet, and sat down again at the instrument. He played the first line of the tune, then nodded to her, and Annie sang.

At the end, the young man was still for a moment, and his face was sad. Then he said, 'What's your name, child?'

'Annie, sir.'

'You've a sweet voice, Annie. It reminds me –'

The door opened and an older man came in. He stopped in astonishment, frowning. 'John, what is going on? Who is this?'

A servant was summoned, and Annie found herself taken to the kitchen by a disapproving woman in a black dress and white apron who gave her some soup and bread as instructed. 'What can the young master be thinking of,' she tutted. 'Bringing young females into the house, and his poor wife not dead a twelvemonth.'

'What is his name?' Annie asked, still enchanted by the music.

'John Clerk, the same as his father.'

'Did his wife used to sing?'

'Aye, she'd a beautiful voice, God rest her.'

'Why did she die?'

'In childbirth. And that's enough questions, young miss. You can sleep in the hayloft, but I want you gone in the morning.'

'I will be,' said Annie with dignity. 'I have things to do.'

She set out at dawn the next day, wishing she could have

said goodbye to John Clerk and thanked him for his kindness. She wondered why the servant woman had been so disapproving. Perhaps she liked being part of the grand house and all its riches, and thought it was her duty to keep other common people out.

The growing daylight was clear and rosy, and Annie soon came to a cluster of small houses, then to a wooden structure where a great wheel turned. She stopped to look, and saw that the wheel was driven by water pouring over its blades from a high channel. A long rope was winding round the spindle which the wheel turned, and a huge bucket came slowly up from a hole in the ground. It, too, was full of water, which a man tipped out. Then he reversed the wheel's turning and sent the bucket down again.

Annie frowned. Why use water to raise water which was then thrown away? The man laughed at her puzzled face. 'Have you never seen a water-gin before?'

When Annie shook her head, he went on, 'It brings the water out of the mine that's underneath here. We have to keep the shafts drained, you see. As it is, the men are knee-deep half the time.'

'My father's a miner,' Annie said, 'I came to find him. His name is Tam Weir, from Maxwellheugh. It's near Kelso.'

'I never heard tell of him,' said the man. 'But keep asking, lassie. Someone will know.' The bucket came up, and he emptied it again.

Annie walked on. A mile or two down the road, coal-blackened women were coming from a dark tunnel-mouth, bending double under their loads. Big baskets of coal were strapped to their backs, and one strap went round the fore-head, to stop the weight from slipping backwards. There were children among them, harnessed like ponies to heavy skips of coal that scraped their way over the rough, coal-strewn surface on runners. Again and again, Annie put her question, but got no more than an exhausted shake of the head from the dust-begrimed people.

As the daylight faded, the working day came to an end

and crowds of miners came out of the shafts. They were so totally black that the whites of their eyes gleamed in startling contrast. In the evening light, they seemed to have no features, and Annie wondered if she would recognise her father even if she found him. She pushed the thought away and ran from one group to another, asking if they knew of Tam Weir.

People were disappearing into the small cottages that stood in a joined row on either side of the rough street, and Annie began to despair. She walked on further, catching up with some workers coming from another pit-mouth, and put her question again – and a man said, 'Tam Weir? Aye, he drinks in Bessie Sweeney's, over there.'

Annie went to the door of the ale-house and looked in. The dim, yellowish light of smoky oil lamps made the room as mysterious as a deep pool in which the shapes of dark fish moved, and the fumes of beer and whisky caught at her throat. Could one of these half-visible men be her father? She was not sure, and she dared not go in.

'Who're you wanting?' A boy not much older than Annie paused on the step as he pushed past her. She told him, and he nodded. 'Tam!' she heard him shout. 'Someone for you.'

A black, thin man detached himself from the others and came towards her, his eye-whites glittering in their red-rimmed sockets. 'Annie,' he whispered. 'My wee sparrow.' Then his black arms were round her, and the beery, coal-reeking smell of him enveloped her.

In the weeks that followed, Annie learned about working in the mines. Every man had to have a 'bearer' who would carry the coal he hewed up to the surface. Most bearers were the wives or children of the miners, but those with no family had to hire one.

'Three pence a day,' Tam said. 'It's a lot out of a man's wages.'

'But you won't have to pay it any more,' Annie said. 'I'm going to help you.'

Tam argued, but only weakly. He coughed all the time, and in the morning his dirty hands trembled until he had called at Bessie Sweeney's for a dram of whisky, 'to set me up,' he said.

Like the other children, Annie wore a leather harness across her shoulders, ending in a long strap like a tail. This was hooked to the coal skip. She carried a lighted tallow candle so that she could see her way as she dragged the skip up the steep shaft. Her collar-bones were soon blistered with the rubbing of the harness, and a woman gave her some rags to put under the straps. By the end of the ten-hour day, every muscle and bone of Annie's body ached with exhaustion, and she stumbled home at her father's side more asleep than awake.

One evening she asked, 'When will you have enough money for us to go home?'

Tam could not meet her eyes. 'We cannae go home, lassie,' he said. 'Mine workers are bondsmen. We belong to the pit-owners, like the shovels and picks and baskets. I'd thought at first that I'd just work a few months then run away, but they hunt you down, Annie. Bring you back in chains. You need strength to run. I've nae strength, not now. I'm sorry.'

Annie's dust-rimmed eyes prickled with angry tears, but she put her hand over his and said nothing.

As time went on, she came to understand that anyone paid to work in the mines was a slave. Good money could be earned, but those who paid it could command endless hours of back-breaking work in the airless, half-flooded shafts, and there was no question of challenging their right, for they had bought their workers' freedom.

5

A year went by. Then, one day in early November, Annie was thrown flat on her face by a blast of smoke-filled wind that burst from the shaft behind her. The skip she hauled leapt forward with the force of it and smoke billowed into the sky. People were screaming and choking. A gale of fierce heat followed the blast, and as Annie picked herself up from among the rubble, she thought of the fire that always burned in the pit to keep a draught moving, and knew it must have ignited the dust-filled air. And her father was down there.

Tears were pouring down her filthy face as she began to stumble back into the smoke-filled shaft. A miner caught her by the arm and said, 'Whaur you goin', lassie?'

'My father –'

'It's nae use. Everything's burning down there.' He pushed her before him to the tunnel entrance, rough in his kindness. In the smoky daylight a crowd had gathered, and Isabel, the woman who had given Annie the rags for her shoulders, stepped forward and put an arm round her. 'Come away, my dear,' she said. 'There's nothing we can do here.'

Isabel kept Annie with her for several days, until the bodies, or what could be found of them, were brought out of the mine and buried. Tam was never identified. Nobody said to Annie that he might have been part of those name-less sackfuls that also went to the churchyard. 'He can never have known anything about it,' people told her in a clumsy effort at comfort. 'He must have been right near the explosion, and that's a mercy.'

At the funeral, Annie stood white-faced and silent as the minister spoke his words and the stony, coal-mingled earth was shovelled back on to the coffins. Tam's grave was the mine that had killed him, she thought, and saw again the roughly-nailed timbers that barred its entrance. His memorial was the hill that rose above it, and the eagles that turned and swooped in the clear air.

'Annie, you should leave here,' Isabel said a few days later. 'Don't go as a bearer to some other man. Some of them – well, I wouldnae like a daughter of mine to be with them.' Her own husband had survived the disaster, and he and Isabel were working in another pit, but she had made Annie stay in the house. 'I told them you died with your father,' she said. 'There's folk know otherwise, but they won't let on. You can get away, Annie, no one will be looking for you.'

Still numb with shock and grief, Annie struggled to make sense of the chance she had been given. Yes, she must go – but where? There was snow on the hills now, and she was painfully thin and exhausted; she could not make the long trek back to Kelso. Why was she even thinking of it? She did not know whether Robert had lived or died, and she could not go back to being a burden on him and Margaret. She thought with a sudden longing of the kitchen in the grand house where John Clerk had heard her sing. 'Maybe I could get a job as a servant,' she said.

'Why not?' agreed Isabel. 'You could do that well, you're a good-mannered lassie. Go to Edinburgh – there's fine, big houses there.'

A few days later, scrubbed as clean as she could get and wearing a dress that Isabel had found from somewhere, Annie came down Blackford Hill after a day's walk, and stared at the close-packed roofs and spires of Edinburgh that lay across the moor. She had never seen such a city. The smoke from its hundreds of chimneys drifted up past the castle on its rock, and the houses reached in a solid mass right down to the shores of the loch that bounded it on the north. How many people must live in such a place? Hundreds . . . no, thousands. And she, not yet thirteen, must go down there and try to find a place for herself and work to do. She felt sick with fear at the thought – but her father's voice rang in her mind, strong and full of hope as he'd been before he went to Darien. *You are as good as anyone else . . . It's just a matter of chance.*

Annie took a deep breath, forcing herself to hold her head up and her shoulders back. Then she went on, towards whatever awaited her.

6

Three hours later, it was dark and cold, and the cobbled streets offered no refuge. Ravenously hungry, Annie walked aimlessly along alleys and up and down the stone stairs that linked the city's steep levels, passing ale-houses that roared with life and private doors as tightly closed as if they guarded the dead.

A man stepped from the shadows and caught Annie round the waist with a drunken blether of endearments, and she tore herself away and ran. Her fear was made worse by a loud rattle of drum-beats quite near at hand, and she dived into a dark doorway – then gasped. Someone was there already, a woman who looked like a ragged bundle of dirty clothes. Annie backed away, but the woman caught her arm.

'Did you no' hear the drum?' she said.

'What do you mean, the –' but in the next instant windows burst open in the houses, and amid a yelling of 'Gardy loo!' there was a tossing of filthy liquids – and worse – into the streets.

Annie covered her face with her hands, coughing with the stench, and when she could speak, she spluttered, 'What are they doing?'

The woman stared at her. 'You must be a stranger,' she said. 'It's the slopping-out. Ten o'clock at night, time to empty the chamber pots. The drum's to warn you.'

Annie was appalled. Even in the mining villages, there had been decent middens behind the houses where muck was piled, eventually to be used on the fields as manure. They stank, naturally, but it was better than flinging waste into the streets where people walked. But the city had no fields, she supposed, and no space between its close-packed houses.

'Where are you from, anyway?' the woman asked. 'What are you doing here?'

Annie told her, and admitted that she had nowhere to go.

'You best come back with me, then.' The woman gave a dry cackle of laughter. 'You'll no' be fussy.'

She took Annie to a cellar where people were crowded round a smoky fire, and gave her a hunk of bannock and – after a shouted argument about getting near the fire – a toasted herring.

'You taking an apprentice, Sadie?' a man asked, eyeing Annie. 'No' bad, is she? Nice wee fingers to slip into pockets.'

Annie was too busy eating to take any notice. The warm food was so good that she didn't care if she was among thieves and beggars. They had been kind to her, which was more than could be said for the rest of Edinburgh.

She crept out early the next morning, glad to leave the foul-smelling cellar and its still sleeping occupants. A bright sun was coming up, and the town seemed less frightening. She came to the Grassmarket, where cartloads of hay and straw were being brought in for sale and women stood round the well with their jugs and buckets, gossiping peacefully. From somewhere among the tethered horses a penny whistle was being played, and Annie joined in with the tune, singing as she walked. To her astonishment, a passing man put a coin in her hand. She stopped to look at it, and a beggar woman grinned toothlessly and said, 'A good start to your day, hen.'

Annie walked on. So she had become a beggar. But at least she could offer a sweet tune to those who might give; she was not asking for something for nothing. She began to sing again, walking more slowly now, and looking into the faces of those who passed.

By the time darkness fell, she had three pence – the same as she used to earn for ten hours of bone-aching work in the mine. She had no idea what the money was worth, for her mining wages had been Tam's to keep. Did she have enough for a night's lodging? She was not sure, and the prospect of looking for a bed was daunting. To keep her spirits up, she began to sing again, and did not notice that she was being overtaken by a group of men. As they passed, one of them stopped, feeling in his pocket. Annie glanced at him hopefully – and blushed with a shock of recognition when she saw that it was John Clerk.

He frowned, half-remembering. 'Aren't you the girl – no, it can't be.'

'Yes! At Penicuik. You asked me to sing.' Finding a face she knew in this town of strangers filled Annie with joy.

Clerk's friends were waiting for him, and he waved a hand. 'Go on, I'll catch you up. See you at Patrick Steil's.'

They went ahead, glancing curiously at Annie.

'What happened to you?' Clerk asked. 'My father had intended to speak to you the next day – there were things he wanted to ask. Where have you been?'

Annie started to tell him as she fell into step at his side, and Clerk listened attentively. 'Dear Heaven,' he murmured to himself, 'is this how people live?'

They came to a tavern, and he pushed open the door. Annie stood back, sorry that he was leaving so soon – but his hand was on her shoulder, and she found herself in a warm, bright room that was full of well-dressed men. Annie stared at the silk-lined cloaks and silver buckles, the long wigs and clean white neck-ties, and shrank back in embarrassment. Heads turned to take in her ragged shawl and dirty bare feet, and someone said ironically, 'Are you opening a poor-house, John?'

'You can stop your laughing, Andrew Fletcher,' Clerk retorted. 'I may not be a great man of politics like you, but at least I can see what's going on under my nose.'

'Aye, but these ills will not be cured until Scotland has charge of its own affairs,' Fletcher said. 'This child's poverty is the whole nation's poverty, don't you see?'

'I see she's half starved,' said Clerk. 'Molly, can you find her something to eat?'

The landlord's wife nodded, and within a few minutes,

Annie was in the kitchen with a plate of rabbit stew in front of her.

7

From that day, a new life began. Annie stayed with Patrick and Molly Steil, working in the house and fetching water from the well in exchange for her food and keep. With enough to eat at last, she began to grow and blossom. She was nearly thirteen now, and she soon began to help in the tavern in the evenings – and when the hour grew late and the talk gave way to singing, she delighted the company with her clear voice and endless memory for the old verses.

She came to understand, too, a little of what the men who met there had in common.

'They're against the union,' Molly explained as she sliced leeks for the soup pot.

'What union?'

'The union with England. The English want our two countries to be one. And so do some of our Scots lords who have big estates in England.'

'But why –'

Molly fished a penny from her apron pocket. 'See this? You'd need 12 of these Scottish pennies to make one English one. Twelve Scottish pounds to the English pound. That's how poor we are compared with England. But our fine men down there have English tastes and English expenses. They think they'd be richer if our countries were made the same.'

'And would they be?'

'Heaven knows. Here, chop these carrots for me.'

'We're poor because of Darien, aren't we?' said Annie, picking up her knife. 'And the bad harvests.' She knew all about that.

'Aye, but because of the English as well,' Molly said. 'They want Scotland safe under their control. Small and poor as we are, they're scared of us.'

'Why?'

'They never know what we'll get up to. We're friendly with France, for a start – always have been. And England is at war with France. What if we let the French armies come across Scotland to attack England from the north? They'd be hard put to it to defend two fronts at once – it would split their forces.'

'But why would we?' Annie asked, shovelling carrots into the pot.

'Why not?' said Molly fiercely. 'What have the English ever done for us except block our trade and invade our country and kill our people? They want to keep us poor, because that way we have no power. We hoped things would be better when William died and Queen Anne came to the throne, but she's as bad.'

'They say she had eighteen children and they all died,' said Annie. 'Poor lady.'

Molly snorted. 'She couldn't even get *that* right,' she

said. 'Now everyone's quarrelling over who'll be king or queen when she dies. The Jacobites say it has to be their beloved James Edward Stuart, who's been away in France all these years, but the English want some woman called Sophia. What's to happen at the end of it I just don't know.'

John Clerk did not come to the tavern often, but one morning he walked in and said, 'Annie, will you do something for me?'

'Yes, willingly,' Annie felt she owed him a debt she could never repay.

He gave her a long, thin package. 'Carry it carefully,' he said. 'It's a flute.' His snub-nosed, boyish face held an expression somewhere between mischief and resentment. 'My father says I must marry again. Give up "this music nonsense" as he calls it, get back to my law studies. I suppose he's right. He's getting old, and I will have to step into his shoes, be a responsible citizen. So this flute is to go to a young woman, Annie, and she will not be able to play it – not until she takes out the letter that's rolled up inside it.' Mischief won, and he smiled briefly. 'Maybe she never will.'

Annie looked at the name written on the flute's wrappings. 'Susannah Kennedy.'

Clerk seemed surprised. 'So you can read?'

'Yes, I learned in Kelso. Mr Lockhart taught me.'

'Lockhart,' he said thoughtfully. 'There's a Lockhart who comes in here – a friend of Fletcher's. I wonder.'

At Susannah Kennedy's house, the servant who took the package from Annie wore white stockings and a powdered wig, and did not smile. The grand front door had closed before she turned to leave the step, and she thought, I hope he marries someone else.

On her way back, Annie found the Grassmarket crowded with people, all staring up at a rough platform, above which rose a stout wooden frame. She stopped, unable to push her way through, and saw a slenderly-built lad being hustled on to the platform. His hands were bound and his face was as white as chalk, but he held his head up bravely, and Annie heard him say, 'I did no more than speak the truth as I know it.' A black-clad minister muttered a prayer, then the boy was half-lifted, half-pushed on to a stool so that he stood higher than his captors. Annie had hardly realised what was going to happen before a noose of rope suspended from the frame was placed about his neck and the stool kicked away.

Annie screamed, and a low rumble of anger rose from the crowd as the boy's body dangled on the rope, jerking like a hooked fish. She turned to run, sobbing with shock, but tripped on the cobbles and almost fell. Strong hands caught her and held her steady, and she found that a dark-haired boy of about the same age as the one who had just died was standing before her, his face mirroring her own revulsion.

'Come away,' he said and took her hand, towing her behind him as he made his way through the crowd.

'What did he do?' Annie gasped when the boy stopped

in a side street. 'Why did they –'

'Spoke against the English queen,' said the boy bitterly. 'As do many of us. That treacherous witch has forgotten she is a Stewart of Scottish blood, even if she did marry some stupid prince of Denmark. She treats her own people like a rabble of beggars. There now,' he added. 'For saying that, I could be the one with a noose round his neck. The lad back there was unlucky, that's all.'

Annie's thoughts buzzed like flies in her mind. For the first time, she saw that the political talk in Patrick Steil's tavern was not just empty debate. These were things that people died for. She stared into the boy's grey eyes, and with great gentleness, he gathered her close to him. She buried her head in his shoulder, and, for a moment at least, felt safe.

8

The grey-eyed boy was called Allan Ramsay, and after that day he came to the tavern often, to see Annie and also because he was excited to find that so many famous men met there. 'I'm just an apprentice to a wig-maker,' he said to Annie, 'But I'll no' spend all my life ornamenting the heads of the gentry. I want to write, Annie – to make plays and poems that will live after I am forgotten.'

Annie laughed, but secretly she respected his grand ideas. Why not? She had met George Lockhart, who was indeed a nephew of the Kelso dominie, and he had talked to her a lot, bringing welcome news of Robert and Margaret, who were surviving in their own resolute way. Robert, as

Annie had feared, could no longer shoe horses, but his skill as a general iron-smith enabled him to make a living from more humdrum work of turning out hinges and bolts – and recently the Kelso minister had asked him to provide scrolled ironwork for the church doors, replacing the old ones that had worn away.

George Lockhart spoke of other things, as well. He explained that most of the men who came to Patrick Steil's were members of the Country party, Scottish patriots who were opposed to the union with England, but he himself was a Jacobite, and they as a political party were known as the Cavaliers.

'Jacobus,' Annie remembered. 'Latin for James. So they want the true descendants of King James on the Scottish throne.'

Lockhart laughed. 'My uncle taught you well,' he said. Then he added, 'Do you know, Annie, the English have not yet laid down that all their children should have the right to education? With us, it's been the law since 1633 that children must go to school – even though it's taken a long time to enforce it.'

'I'm glad I'm Scottish,' Annie said.

She came to understand that the leader of the Country party was James Douglas, the Earl of Hamilton, a dark, elegant man with a charming smile. 'A born leader,' Lockhart said. 'Clever, astute, powerful – but he has big estates in England. It may be that his Scottish patriotism is not as strong as his need for English money.'

Andrew Fletcher shared Lockhart's doubts. There were often fierce disagreements between him and Hamilton, and one night he burst out that the leader had more faces than a crowd at a hanging. Hamilton smiled, apparently unruffled, but his eyes were wary.

Annie quite often ran messages and delivered letters, but when Hamilton gave her a letter to take to an Edinburgh house one day, she looked at the name uneasily. Wasn't the Earl of Mar a member of the Court party, in favour of union? Their leader, the Duke of Queensberry, effectively ruled Scotland as the Queen's agent, and could not wait to make the two countries one.

'Don't deliver it,' Allan urged when Annie met him by the well and showed him the sealed letter.

She shook her head. 'I must,' she said. But Allan told Fletcher, and there was a huge row in the tavern that night. Hamilton listened with weary tolerance while accusations raged.

'Force and passion will get you nowhere, my friends,' he said. 'Trade is the way of the world – and before you condemn me, bear in mind that I always get a little more than I give.'

Fletcher snorted with contempt, but there were cautious nods of agreement among some of the others. Annie, wiping tables and covertly watching, was grateful to Andrew Fletcher for saying he had intercepted her with the letter and insisted on seeing the address on it, because of his suspicion of double-dealing. But her own concerns were nothing compared with the sense of impending disaster which hung over the men in the tavern. It seemed for the first time that union with England was going to come, and nothing the Scottish patriots could do would stop it.

Over the next months, things got worse. The captain, mate and gunner of an English ship called the Worcester were hanged at Leith, in Scottish fury because an ex-Darien ship had been impounded in London and accused of piracy – and the argument over who should rule after Queen Anne raged on. Determined to bring the Scots to heel, the London government passed an Act demanding their acceptance of Sophia, the daughter of the king of Bohemia. Through her mother, she was the granddaughter of James VI, but the Jacobites protested that James Edward Stewart had a closer claim, being the son of James VII. This was true – but Sophia was a Protestant, and the English wanted no truck with a Catholic Stewart king. Their Act declared an ultimatum. If the Scots went on objecting to Sophia, all trade between England and Scotland would be stopped.

No cattle would cross the border, no wool or linen would be imported. And, what was more, no Scot living in England would be allowed to inherit property.

'What does that mean?' Annie asked when Allan told her the news.

'It means our Scots lords who have married into English families and own estates down there will not be able to leave them to their sons,' Allan said. 'Within a generation, they will lose all their fine houses and their wealth. England is going to treat them like aliens, with no rights there at all.'

Annie stared at him as an awful understanding settled in her mind. 'They won't hold out against that,' she said. 'Mr Fletcher's cause is lost.' And Allan nodded wordlessly.

That evening, the men in the tavern were grim-faced, and Lockhart said to Fletcher, 'The English will win with this, Andrew. They have our Scots lords wriggling.'

'Money,' said Fletcher bitterly. 'In the end, it's the only weapon that counts. Look at Paterson, who started the

Darien scheme. A good Scots patriot, you'd think. But now he's the queen's lap dog, fat with English cash.'

'I fear the worst,' said Lockhart.

In the Scottish parliament soon afterwards, on an evening when most of the members had gone home, assured that there would be no more business that night, Hamilton proposed that Scottish MPs should be appointed directly by the queen. It would be simpler, he said, and save a lot of political wrangling. The jubilant Court party seized its chance, and the motion was carried by eight votes.

Fletcher, who had voted against it, broke the news to the aghast listeners in the tavern. 'So now we are robbed of the right to elect our own Members,' he said. 'Our parliament will be made up of the queen's picked men.' He stared round the silent room, and his words fell heavily. 'From this day we may date the commencement of Scotland's ruin.'

9

The general public knew nothing of what had happened, and wherever Hamilton went he was cheered as the leader who would defend Scotland's independence. But the shadows were gathering. The new parliament agreed in principle to union with England, and in the months while the details were worked out, ordinary Scottish people began to understand that this was the end of Scotland as an independent nation. Dismay turned to fury. Long lists of signatures protesting against the union were sent to Parliament, and rioting broke out all over the country. A copy of the Treaty of Union was burned in the streets of Dumfries, and a ragtag army of outraged citizens gathered itself to march on Edinburgh. Hamilton hurried to meet them. This was not the time, he told them. They should hold their protest until the present negotiations had failed – if indeed they did. He had the whole matter in hand, he assured them. They must trust him. So the people, beguiled by his handsome face and easy smile, halted their attack.

The Court party had no need to waste charm on the populace. In their view, commoners were there to work and to do as they were told. As the Earl of Mar remarked, they were 'meddling in matters that did not concern them, and in which they had no right to meddle.' But since it was only landowners and noblemen who had the right to vote, Annie thought, how else were people to make their opinions known? The answer soon became obvious. Mar was shouted at and reviled whenever he ventured into the streets, and said he feared for his life.

A few days later, English troops began to gather on the border.

'Surely it can't mean war?' Annie said, horrified.

Allan shook his head. 'The English can't afford a war, they're already fighting France. No, the soldiers are there to protect men like Mar – but the threat is there.'

'The stick and the carrot,' put in Molly, overhearing. 'If we go along like a nice, obedient donkey, they'll repay the Darien debt, and all the Scots lords who lost money will be rich again. If we don't, then it's no money, no trade and probably a war as well. Some choice, huh?'

All through that uneasy winter, soldiers garrisoned in Edinburgh castle patrolled the streets. The Provost of Glasgow had to flee for his life as an angry mob of Scottish patriots took over the city, and an Englishman called Daniel Defoe who was spying for the queen reported that Edinburgh was in a 'most dreadful uproar'.

On May 1st, 1707, Scotland and England became one, to the relief of the nobility and the despair of the people.

'Don't go out, Annie,' begged Molly. 'There's a riot going on. They say the Duke of Queensberry was pelted with stones.'

But Annie was too grieved and angry to stay indoors. She had seen Andrew Fletcher ride away that morning, perhaps for ever. With one foot in the stirrup, he had turned to look at the friends who stood round, begging him to stay in Scotland. 'It is only fit for the slaves who sold it,' he said. Then he mounted his horse and was gone.

In the yelling surge of people that filled the High Street, Annie was glad of Allan's warm hand grasping hers. 'Soldiers!' someone shouted, and she glimpsed the flash of sword-blades ahead of her. Stones were flying, and Allan suddenly staggered, clutching his head. A flaring brand carried by one of the mob showed Annie that blood was oozing between Allan's fingers. She steered him into a doorway, as fearful as she had been on that first night in Edinburgh so many years ago. 'Let me see,' she said.

A deep split on Allan's brow was bleeding fast, filling his eye and running down his cheek. 'It's all right,' he said, rubbing it with the back of his hand. 'Just a cut. Someone didn't find the right target.'

'Aye, that's the way of it,' said Annie bitterly. 'Targets missed and innocent people hurt.' She was almost in tears. 'What's the matter with us, Allan? Scot against Scot, Protestant against Catholic, the rich who want their money against the poor who want their freedom.'

Allan put his arm round her, careless of injury and blood. 'Annie,' he said, 'don't lose faith. One day it won't be just the noblemen whose voices are heard. People like you and me will have our say, and nobody will tell us we have no right. It's going to happen, I'm sure of it.'

You are as good as anyone else, Annie remembered. Tam lay in the black earth of Midlothian and her mother in Maxwellheugh where so many had died of starvation, but Annie was their daughter, and their spirit lived on in her. She raised her head from Allan's shoulder and smiled at him. 'Who knows?' she said. 'Perhaps one day, we'll be a nation again.'

Allan smiled back at the sight of her blood-smudged

face. 'Just look at you,' he said. 'Reckless girl.'

Annie shrugged and kissed him. Then Allan took her hand and they made their way through the shouting, battling crowd to the well in the Grassmarket, where they washed themselves clean in the cold, sweet water of Scotland.

Life in Eighteenth-century Scotland

in Lowland Scotland died, or moved away if they could.

Families were usually allocated a different strip of land each year so that everyone took a turn at farming the best or the worst land. This was called the 'runrig' system. Where tenants had the same land year after year it was 'fixed runrig'; just occasionally, a group of peasants would rent and farm a bigger block of land communally, and this was 'rundale'. No single peasant family could afford to own a ploughing team of horses or oxen, so these were bought and used communally. The ploughed 'infield' grew oats, peas, beans and a form of barley called 'bere', and kale was grown close to the houses as a garden crop. Beyond this ploughed land was the 'outfield', where cattle and sheep grazed. These tended to be small and skinny because each peasant was tempted to raise as many as he could and there were too many of them on the rough moorland. This was why the Highland cattle, grazing on miles of mountain-side in the north, were of much better quality.

During the famine years, the starving families were forced to slaughter their beasts so as to have something to eat, but the final tragedy was the using of precious seed-corn for food, leaving nothing to sow in the following spring. The landlords, too, were suffering, having no produce to sell, but their response was often to put the rent up, which made things even worse for the starving peasants. The landlord held absolute authority over his tenants, and could hand out punishments for any misbehaviour. Causing a disturbance or failing to attend church on Sunday could land the offender in the stocks, and in the harsher Highlands, the clan chieftains could order a flogging or even a hanging.

Education

Some landlords accepted their responsibility to provide local schools, and would fine their peasants for failing to send their children, but others were reluctant to undertake this duty, which cost them the teacher's wages and the provision of a school building. As early as 1496, James IV had ordered that the sons of barons and freeholders should be sent to school by the age of eight or nine to study Latin, Art and Law, and by

1633 the Scottish parliament had laid down that every parish must have its school, open to all children. The peasants had to pay a small contribution for this (as well as sending a peat for the school fire), and it tended to become impossible in times of hardship. Working children such as those in the mines or the salt industry were completely overlooked. Those who went to school had an eight-hour day, and many had a long walk at either end of it, but if they were studious, there were bursaries available to send them to University. The sons of the gentry tended to ignore the Scottish universities, established in St Andrews and the major cities since the fifteenth century, and thought it much superior to study abroad.

Drove roads

The Highlands, being mountainous and wild, were never cultivated as intensively as Annie's Lowland area, so although life was harder, they were always able to graze their hardy black cattle on miles of open moorland. These cattle were driven south across Scotland and over the border for sale in England,

and it was this traffic that formed the drove roads. The drovers Annie met had come through Kelso because they had to pay a tax either there or in Jedburgh for exporting their cattle to England (which they resented bitterly). There was a desperate need for better roads, and ever since 1617 successive Scottish parliaments had been trying to link ports and market towns with a hard-surfaced road system – but the landlords would not contribute to the cost. It was only after the union of 1707, when the British government wanted to send in troops to put down the Jacobite risings, that roads as we know them were at last built.

Mining

The mining industry was expanding rapidly at about the time of Darien and afterwards. Monasteries such as Newbattle Abbey had for many years been using coal dug from their own grounds, but by 1707 the annual output was around 500,000 tonnes. The peat banks were running out, and the Lowlands were almost stripped of trees because of the need for fuel in the salt industry and the developing towns.

At first, the pits were shallow, but as the coal near the surface was used up, deeper shafts were dug, reached by ladders. Women used to climb up these, carrying the unbelievable load of 1½ cwt – nearly 80 kg! A man delivering coal to a house today will seldom carry more than 25 kg.

Hundreds of children worked in the mines as Annie did. They carried a 'half load' weighing a mere 40 kg, and their lives were appallingly hard. In West Lothian a quarter of all mine workers were under 13 years old, and it was not uncommon for them to work from 5am to 5pm, and sometimes all night. Miners were serfs, the property of the pit owner to use as he liked, and the bondage system was not abandoned until 1799 – and then only because it was becoming impossible to recruit workers.

Edinburgh

Edinburgh in Annie's day was much smaller than it is now. The New Town had not been built, and the North Loch, or Nor'

Loch as it was called, filled the space now bordered by Prince's Street, where the railway runs into Waverley Station. The city was a huddle of close-packed houses clustered round the castle, contained within its city walls, with gates to close against invaders. Modern street names such as Canongate remember this.

There was a chronic shortage of water, and the Nor' Loch stank because of the offal and refuse thrown into it. But in 1678 a conduit had been built to bring water from Coniston Springs, and several more wells had been built in the '80s. Even so, 'caddies' earned themselves a living by carrying water in from Holyrood, which was outside the city wall. They would also, for a small fee, go ahead of citizens at the dangerous time of 10pm, shouting, 'Haud your hand!' – and getting the slops poured on them if the housewife upstairs did not hear the warning.

There was a postal service of sorts. Twice a week, men known as 'post-boys' would leave Edinburgh at midnight to walk to Glasgow with their sacks of letters, arriving the following evening. It was an expensive service, and couriers like Annie were commonly used.

People Annie knew

Annie herself could be any one of many girls who lived as she did, but the men who met at Patrick Steil's tavern (which was a real place) were people famous in their own time. Allan Ramsay became known as a great poet and opened Edinburgh's first bookshop, and although Mr Lockhart, the dominie of Kelso, may not have existed, George Lockhart of Carnwath most certainly did. The outspoken Andrew Fletcher of Saltoun was a notable patriot of his day, and James Douglas, fourth Duke of Hamilton, was indeed the leader of the Country party, although he played a double game throughout his life. 'I have done Her Majesty signal service,' he wrote to James Graham after his proposal that the queen alone should appoint Scottish MPs to their own parliament. He was finally killed in a duel in 1712, and many people said it was a put-up job to get rid of him. Sir John Clerk, father of the musician who asked Annie to sing for him, said Hamilton was a man who 'would comply with anything on a suitable encourage-ment.' In other words, he sided with whoever paid best.

The younger John Clerk had displeased his father by going to Rome to study music with the famous Corelli instead of becoming a lawyer. All the rest of his story is true, including the note in the flute – but Susannah Kennedy would not have him. She could pick and choose, perhaps, for a rhyme of the time remarked:

> *Frae Wigtown to the town of Ayr,*
> *Port Patrick to the Cruives of Cree,*
> *Nae man need think for to bide there*
> *Unless he court a Kennedy.*

John Clerk married elsewhere and became an architect – but Scotland lost a great musician.

John Erskine, the Earl of Mar, who spoke so disparagingly

about the views of the common people, changed his mind about the virtues of union with England after it came about in 1707. He voted against it when there was a proposal in the House of Lords to return to separate countries (lost by only four votes), and became a keen Jacobite. He was derisively known as 'Bobbing John' for the way he hopped from one side to the other.

Daniel Defoe is best known to us as the author of *Robinson Crusoe*, but Annie knew of him as a rather theatrical English spy who dressed up as a fish merchant or a glassblower in order to go among common people and find out what they thought.

Scottish history

Until 1603, about 80 years before Annie was born, Scotland was a separate country from England, with its own kings and queens. The Stewart family had produced a line of King Jameses who had ruled for many years – but the trouble began when James IV married Margaret, the sister of the English king, Henry VIII. It seemed a good idea at the time, hopefully bringing the warring kingdoms closer together, but Henry's Tudor family died out in 1603 with his younger daughter, the childless Queen Elizabeth, leaving no English prince to inherit the throne. Because of the marriage between Margaret and James a couple of generations back, James VI of Scotland was by far the closest relative, so he added the English crown to his Scottish one, becoming England's James I. This Union of Crowns laid the ground for a move towards a closer union which would combine the governments of the two countries. Much happened, however, before this came about, and the combined countries ran through five rulers before ending up with Queen Anne of Annie's time. Each of these monarchs added a little to the dilemma that was facing the men in Patrick Steil's tavern.

- **Charles I** was the son of James VI/I. He ruled from 1625 to 1649, and was so arrogant and unpleasant that he provoked a revolution and got himself executed.

- **Oliver Cromwell** followed, who was not a king at all, but a severe Puritan leader determined to purge the country of what he saw as its decadent Royalist Catholicism. He attacked Scotland because it would not recognise him as leader and had instead crowned Charles II, son of the executed king, as their monarch.

- **Charles II** was also crowned by the English, but not until after Cromwell's death in 1658. He sympathised with the Catholics, but England was still strongly Protestant, and Charles was compelled to agree that no Roman Catholic should hold office. He was a man who liked to enjoy himself, and had at least 16 illegitimate children but no legal ones, and after his death he was succeeded by his younger brother, James II, who was also James VII of Scotland.

- **James VII/II** horrified everyone by secretly marrying his mistress, Anne Hyde, and by equally secretly converting to Catholicism. After his first wife's death he married the ardently Catholic Mary of Modena. He never set foot in Scotland as a ruling king, and was hated for his reign of terror which sought to reimpose the Catholic religion.

Rebellion rose, and James fled to France and never came back. His son, James Edward, had an obvious claim to the throne, and was known as the Old Pretender, backed by the Jacobites. James Edward was followed in turn by the Young Pretender, his own son, Charles Edward.

Meanwhile, there was determination both in Scotland and England that Catholicism would not return to being the official religion, so when James VII/II fled, there was a need to find a new, Protestant monarch. James VII/II's daughter, Mary, had married William, the Dutch Prince of Orange, so this couple was the obvious choice.

- **William and Mary** ruled during Annie's childhood – hence 'King William's ill years'. He was a boring, serious man, doggedly set on rooting out Catholicism. James II was still the legal monarch of Ireland, so William (known to Orangemen as 'King Billy') attacked and defeated him at the Battle of the Boyne. Determined to subdue the Scottish Highlanders, whom he knew to retain their old Catholic sympathies, William required all clan chieftains to swear an oath of allegiance to him. When the leader of the MacDonalds was late in doing this, William sent in troops who massacred the clan in their homeland of Glencoe – for which he was never forgiven. It was partly in the aftermath of this that he agreed to the Darien venture, hoping to curry some favour in Scotland, although he in fact made sure it would not succeed.

William died in 1702 after his horse stumbled over a molehill and threw him. The Jacobites drank a gleeful toast to the mole, 'the little gentleman in black velvet', but the question of who should succeed the dead king was a vexed one. The exiled Stewart Pretenders were Catholic, and it was only the Jacobites who backed the claim of first James Edward and then Charles Edward. A Protestant monarch had to be found.

- The choice fell on **Anne**, second daughter of James VII/II. She had married Prince George, brother of the Danish king – a nonentity of a man whom nobody took seriously. Poor Anne was exhausted by constant and ever-unsuccessful child-bearing, and she was acutely aware that after the death of her last son, there was no English or Scottish heir apart from her half-brother, James Edward Stewart. She tried hard to persuade him to renounce his Catholicism so that he would be an acceptable heir to the throne, but without success. The English had settled on the German princess, Sophia of Hanover, whose family was descended from James VI of Scotland, and this was what caused such dissent in Scotland at the time of the Act of Union. Although the Scots were predominantly Protestants of one kind or another, few of them wanted to be ruled by a queen so foreign to their country.

In the event, the 70-year-old Sophia died a few months before Queen Anne herself, and her eldest son came to the throne of England and Scotland as George I.

The Act of Union and its aftermath

On 1 May 1707, the Act of Union came into force, and the Scottish parliament ceased to exist. There were 45 Scottish

MPs in the House of Commons in London, and 16 Scottish peers in the House of Lords, but Scotland no longer ran its own affairs.

For Annie and people like her, the immediate effects were bad. Scotland was dragged into England's war against France, and as a result, trade between France and Scotland became impossible. It was hard to sell cattle and other goods to the English, too, because heavy taxes were imposed. The Scottish MPs at Westminster were mocked for their accents, and Sir John Clerk roared at his English colleagues to mind their manners after a snide comment about his Scots pronunciation of the word 'water' as 'watter'. He and the other Scots were given to understand that Scotland had been *bought* by the English for the £400,000 of Darien debt repayment – and it was evident that no more money was to be laid out. A plan to build a road to the Highlands so that timber could be exported fell through because England preferred to go on getting timber from Norway and America, and the herring industry nearly collapsed through the punishingly high tax on salt. It was hardly surprising that men like the Earl of Mar began to regret their support for the union.

The Country party had lost its battle to keep Scotland independent, and the main force of dissent now became the Jacobites, who continued to work and plan for restoring a Stewart king to Scotland. Hamilton, ex-leader of the Country party, joined them, and in 1708, just a year after the union, he helped to bring the Old Pretender in a fleet of French vessels to the Firth of Forth. The attempt fizzled out after only four days, largely due to appalling weather, but Hamilton was imprisoned, and so was Fletcher, who had had nothing to do with it.

Hamilton wriggled his way out of trouble and became a favourite at the House of Lords, rising to the position of privy councillor. He was just about to become ambassador to France when he was killed in a very suspect duel with Lord Mohun.

The Jacobites did not give up. Lockhart was imprisoned in Edinburgh Castle for his part in a rising in 1715, and Andrew Fletcher died in Paris the following year. 'Lord have mercy on my poor country that is so barbarously oppressed,' he said with his last breath.

Thirty years passed before things finally came to a head. In 1745 the Jacobites brought the Young Pretender, 'Bonnie Prince Charlie', back from France. The army he raised invaded England and got all the way to Derby before being driven back and defeated at the appalling blood-bath of Culloden. Charles Edward went into hiding in the Highlands until he at last escaped to France, and he is still remembered in such songs as 'Will Ye No' Come Back Again?' and 'Charlie is My Darling' – not to mention the famous Skye Boat Song, 'Carry the man who is born to be king, over the sea to Skye'.

For their support of the Young Cavalier, as Charles Edward was also known, the Highlanders were brutally punished. The Duke of Cumberland, whose savage assault on the Scots at Culloden had earned him the name of 'The Bloody Butcher', set about subduing the clansmen for ever. The chieftains were stripped of their powers and reduced to mere landlords, and the wearing of the tartan plaid was forbidden. No Highlander could carry arms, on pain of death, and an ancient way of life was lost for ever.

Despite all this, the Scots gradually began to win respect for their business judgement and their courage. Trade at last opened up for them, and there is now hardly a country in the world that does not have Scottish families descended from the pioneers who went out to start new enterprises. The union brought peace between England and Scotland after centuries of strife, and many people in both countries believe that it was the best solution to a problem that had become impossible to solve in any other way.

History lives on, however. The old divisions which, as Annie said, set Scot against Scot are still there. The Scottish National Party is the natural continuation of Fletcher's Country party, and the supporters of the union who were once the Court party are now mostly Conservative, with the more recent Labour movement taking in almost all shades of opinion. The religious divide continues to exist, and flares into angry debate from time to time, and there are fundamental differences between Highlands and Lowlands and between the Celtic people of the west and the more Viking-influenced people of the east. And the argument about Scotland's independence is as alive as ever.

The New Scottish Parliament

On 12 May 1999, a Scottish Parliament was elected again, after fewer than 300 years of being combined with England. It does not bring total independence – that remains the next big question to be tackled – but it is a tremendous assertion of Scotland's right to be in charge of her own affairs. And on the football terraces, in defiance of all official disapproval, the crowds sing the anthem which they have made their own. The words of the folk song, written by Roy Williamson of The Corries, echo the hope Annie expressed when she stood beside Allan in the Grassmarket on that night in 1707:

But we can still rise now
And be the nation again.